The Day We Danced in Underpants

by Sarah Wilson
Illustrations by Catherine Stock

TRICYCLE PRESS
Berkeley | Toronto

DISCARD

One bright and breezy summer's day
an invitation came our way
to picnic with the King of France,
his court, his cows, his cats, his plants!

So Papa bought a pair of pants,
sunny, dappled, dancing pants,
and took me off to travel France
with two big dogs and three wild aunts.

A musical bunch, by day and night,
we danced through France, a *jolly* sight,
until with every swoop and spin
poor Papa's pants began to thin.

On picnic day, the air dawned sweet.
We overdressed from head to feet.

We sewed on bells. We ribboned dogs.
We started out with jigs and jogs ...

and then the sun began to roast
until we felt like buttered toast!
My ruffled aunts, weighed down by laces,
pulled off shoes and mopped their faces.

We reached the palace, drooped like roses,
dogs on shoulders, sun-burned noses.
Papa smiled and bravely bowed,
politely as tight pants allowed.

The court was waiting, gates flung wide,
while courtiers welcomed us inside ...

My three delighted aunts cried, "Oooo!"
as pages rushed with great ado
to brush our dogs and lead us on
down marble steps to sprawling lawn.

Our lunch was in a shady glade
with chairs and tables lushly laid,
with plates of melting French eclairs,
and hedges trimmed to look like bears.

We joined the King, our royal host
while counselors followed, stiff as posts.
"We're all as boiled as codfish stew,"
one whispered low. "Aren't *you* warm, too?"

The King and Queen each took their place
and all was quiet for the grace.

Then Papa tried to take his chair and …

BRRRRRRPT!!

we heard a *thunderous* tear!

Five choristers about to sing
were pelted with a *zip-zap-zing*
as buttons shot from here to there,
and we saw Papa's UNDERWEAR!

A moustache twitched. A necklace popped.
Wigs fell askew. Gold platters dropped.
The startled King stood by, amazed.
His courtiers gasped, their eyebrows raised.

The Queen appeared to keep her wits
but then broke into *giggling* fits!
Her footmen tittered. Handmaids squeaked.
Poor Papa blushed from head to feet.

The guests fell down, they laughed so hard.
They rolled across the picnic yard.

The King drew tall and raised his hand
for us to quiet down and stand.
His deep voice boomed, "I NOW DECLARE
WE *ALL* STRIP TO OUR UNDERWEAR!"

And so we peeled to underclothes
to stripes and checks, to hearts and bows,
and gladly let the breezes pass
while dancing on the cool, cool grass.

Musicians struck a merry song.
The afternoon turned bright and long.
The fountains splashed. The statues gleamed.
My three aunts hugged and Papa beamed.

The King, himself, begged, "Please, do stay!" and thanked us for a *splendid* day.

So on I danced with the rosy Queen,
who taught us all a new routine
before the cheering court of France
and all because of Papa's pants!

For a delight of an editor, Abigail Samoun, and our proper but lively and dance-loving French grandmothers, Aida Mary Margaret and Marie-Louise.   —S.W.

Pour Roger et Rachel, mes amis. Que ferions-nous sans des amis?   —C.S.

Tricycle Press
an imprint of Ten Speed Press
PO Box 7123
Berkeley, California 94707
www.tricyclepress.com

Design by Chloe Rawlins
Typeset in Belen and Melanie
The illustrations in this book were rendered in
pen and ink, watercolor, and collage

Library of Congress Cataloging-in-Publication Data

Wilson, Sarah, 1934-
The day we danced in underpants / by Sarah Wilson ; illustrations by Catherine Stock.
p. cm.
Summary: When Papa's pants—worn thin from dancing on his visit to France—split as
he sits down to picnic with the king, the embarrassing moment provides both cooling
and comic relief for the guests, prompting them to take off their hot clothes and dance.
ISBN-13: 978-1-58246-205-9
ISBN-10: 1-58246-205-4
[1. Dance--Fiction. 2. Kings, queens, rulers--Fiction. 3. France--History--Fiction.
4. Humorous stories. 5. Stories in rhyme.] I.
Stock, Catherine, ill. II. Title.
PZ8.3.W698Day 2007
[E]--dc22
2007018172
First Tricycle Press printing, 2008
Printed in Singapore

1 2 3 4 5 6 — 12 11 10 09 08